W9-BVY-883

This story is fun to do as a shadow play. All you need is a bed sheet hung in front of a table, under the table a box filled with ordinary junk from around the house, and behind the table a very strong lamp that casts shadows onto the sheet. The audience, seated in the dark on the other side of the sheet will see only the shadows. When the doctor pulls things out of the box it will look as if the objects are coming from the boy lying on the table. It is better if you make up what to say to go with the objects you use. [Lots of oohing and aahing is good and sound effects can be very funny.] You can also make up tunes as you go along and just sing the whole thing. Then you have an opera-shadow-play.

Has anybody seen my hat?

THIS BOOK IS DEDICATED TO SARA, DORA, ADA, AND THELMA

MOTHER MOTHER I FEEL SICK
SEND FOR THE DOCTOR
QUICK
QUICK
QUICK

A Picture Book and Shadow Play by
REMY CHARLIP & BURTON SUPREE
with pictures by
REMY CHARLIP

Text © Copyright 1966 by Remy Charlip and Burton Supree
Illustrations © Copyright 1966 by Remy Charlip
All rights reserved. Printed in the United States of America
Library of Congress Catalog Card Number 66-13331

PARENTS' MAGAZINE PRESS, NEW YORK

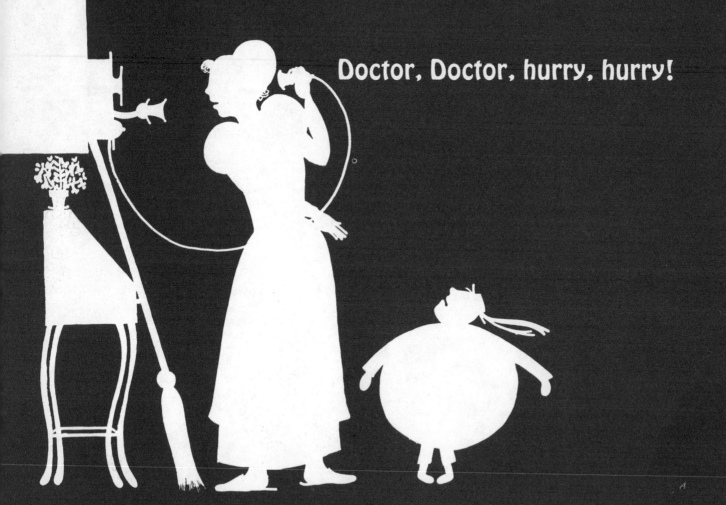

Doctor, Doctor, hurry, hurry!

I'll come right over. Don't you worry.

I've got lotions and potions
and powders and pills.
I've got all kinds of tonics
for all kinds of ills.

Whether itches or sneezes
or twitches or wheezes
or lumps or the mumps
or one single pimple...   I'll cure it! It's simple!

Well, he's gotten so much fatter.
And he has a stomach ache.
Is there some medicine he can take?

Look at him now, he's all green in the face.

I've never seen such a terrible case.

Let's rush him to the hospital this very minute.

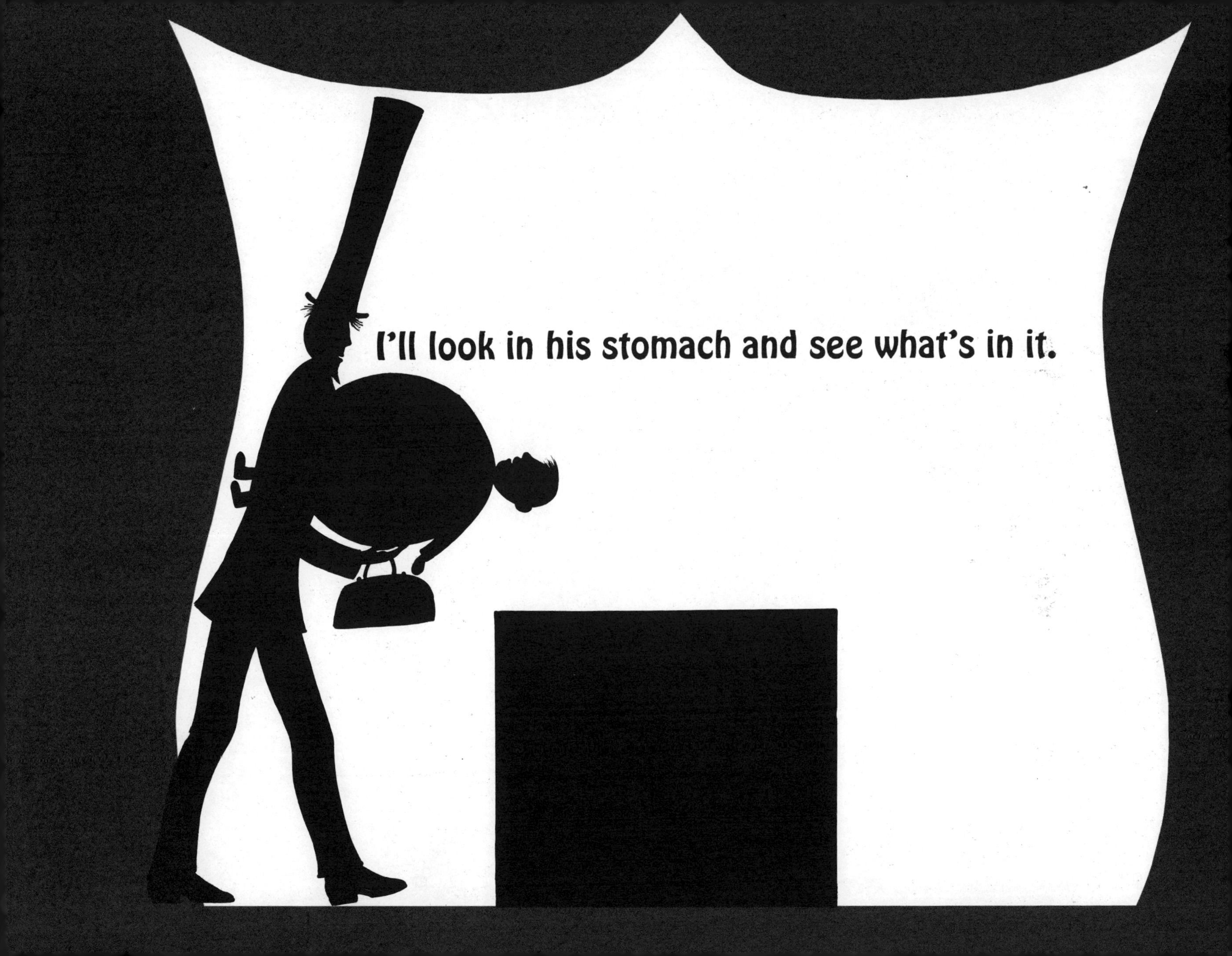

I'll look in his stomach and see what's in it.

Did one green apple cause the trouble
and swell his stomach more than double?

One! Two! Three! And one's a ball!

No wonder he had a stomach ache.

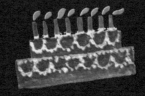

He ate a whole big birthday cake.

He ate the plate!?

That's a rabbit!
And there's my hat!
I knew I didn't lose that hat.

And there are my galoshes and shoes!
I didn't notice they were gone.
I even thought I had them on.

I think we're coming to the end.

Fly down here, my long lost friend.

This
whole
case is
beyond
belief.

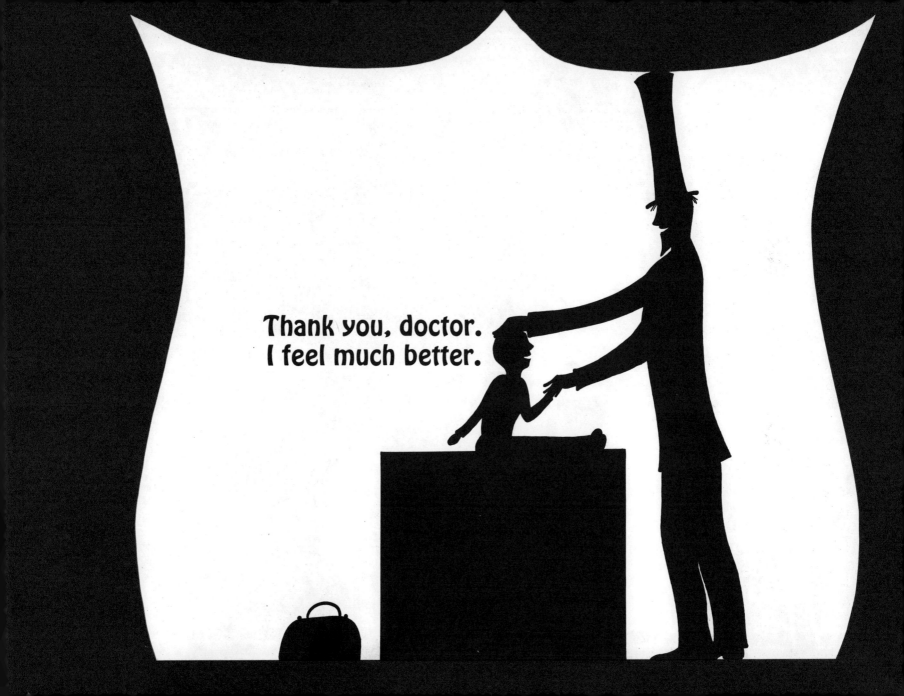

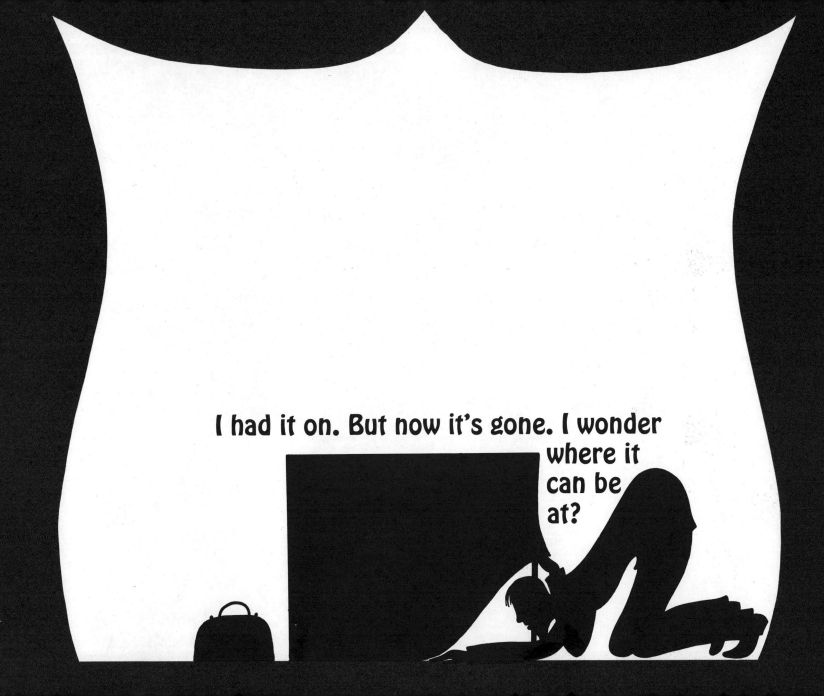

Has anybody seen my hat?